CONTENTS

HEY, THERE! I'M AZALEAH!

I'm eight years old. My life is *amazing*. I live with my family: Mum, Dad, Nia and Tiana.

Mum has her very own restaurant called Avec Amour. That means "with love" in French. She named it that because she adds love to everything she does.

My dad is a lawyer. He sues bad guys for a living. The bad guys are big businesses that do things that hurt other people. But my dad makes them pay. He makes sure they're held responsible.

Tiana is my little sister. She's four years old and pretty cute – most of the time. I like her a lot, even though she comes into my room too much. I also have an older sister named Nia. She's at secondary school and is always in her room. *Always.*

Mum's sister – my Auntie Sam – takes care of us when Mum and Dad are busy. I love Auntie Sam. She's never too tired to play and she loves to do art. She also likes adventures – my favourite!

Apart from my family, there are three main things you should know about me.

1. I'm curious . . . *not* nosy. (Despite what Nia says.)

2. I'm good at solving mysteries – very good.

3. I live in the White House!

OK . . . not the *real* White House. (The president of the United States lives there.) But my house is big and white, plus it has a great big living room and a nice garden. It's just as good as the real White House, if you ask me!

IT'S HARD TO BELIEVE THIS AMAZING LIFE ALL BELONGS TO ME, AZALEAH LANE!

CHAPTER 1
THE BEST DAY EVER

In front of me, a giant, reddish-orange tiger paced back and forth next to a little river. Its mouth was open and its tongue stuck out. I could see its big, sharp teeth, but I wasn't scared.

Somebody else was, though. Behind me, one of my classmates said, "Tigers are scary."

"Some people are afraid of tigers, but if you respect them and follow the zoo rules, they won't hurt you," the tour guide at the zoo explained. "This is Nikita, our six-year-old Amur tiger."

"Why is she alone?" I asked.

"We want her to get used to her new habitat," the zookeeper answered. "She will get to meet her neighbour soon."

I glanced at the enclosure next door. Another tiger lived there. It kept swimming up to a little window to see Nikita.

"I didn't know tigers could swim," I said.

"Most big cats can," the zookeeper replied. "Lions, cheetahs and leopards can all swim, but they tend to avoid water. They're better at hunting on land. Tigers usually live in jungles with lots of wide rivers, so they're good at swimming. The only other big cat that swims well is the jaguar."

I hadn't known that either. There was a lot to learn at the zoo.

"Who's ready to see the giant pandas?" our guide asked.

I waved goodbye to Nikita before I walked away. I wanted to race down the path ahead of the rest of my class, but I knew what would happen if I did: I would be sent to the headteacher. Our teacher, Miss Johnson, had already warned us about staying together.

"Our giant pandas are quite famous," the tour guide continued. "Maybe you've seen them on our webcam."

I nodded. Our class had been been watching the "panda cam" for weeks to get ready for our school trip. The pandas were always eating and taking naps.

Finally the tour guide said, "Let's head over to the panda house."

I fast-walked to the very front of the group, so I was right next to our leader. I wanted to be the first one there.

"Azaleah, wait for me!" my best friend, Rose, called after me.

I didn't wait. I'd been dying to see the pandas all morning. Rose and I had talked about pandas *all* the way from our school to the zoo. Now we were finally going to see them.

At the giant panda enclosure, a zookeeper was waiting for us.

"Welcome to the panda house," she said. "Here at the zoo, one of our goals is conservation. That means making sure all species of animals survive. Pandas are vulnerable. They could become endangered if we don't help them."

I already knew that. We had learned all about endangered animals in class. It was part of our lesson on different habitats and the animals that lived in them.

Our tour guide had also mentioned it. She'd said that tigers were "critically endangered". The zoo was working very hard to save them.

"Pandas in zoos can live to be more than thirty years old," the zookeeper continued. "They spend up to sixteen hours a day eating. When they're not eating, they're sleeping."

In the enclosure, a panda stared at us and took a bite of bamboo. I liked the way the panda just sat there while it ate. It reminded me of how my sisters and I sat on the floor and ate liquorice when we watched films at home.

The zookeeper said, "Pandas sometimes make barking noises to communicate. Who can tell me the natural habitat of a giant panda?"

I raised my hand, and the zookeeper pointed at me.

"Giant pandas live in the mountains in China," I announced. "They live in forests with lots of moisture and plenty of bamboo."

The zookeeper gave me a thumbs-up. "That's right," she said.

After a few more minutes, Miss Johnson smiled at the zookeeper. "Thank you for talking to us," she said.

One of the pandas climbed down from a tree and started rolling around on the grass. The class giggled.

Miss Johnson turned to face us. "We've

learned a lot about natural habitats today," she said. "This has given me a good idea for your next art project. You can all make a model scene of an animal habitat that we saw today."

I grinned. I loved art, and I really loved a challenge. I *definitely* wanted to make a model scene of an animal habitat.

Miss Johnson kept talking. "If you bring your model to school on Monday," she continued, "you will earn extra science points. You will also get to display your work at parents' evening."

This was the best day *ever*. Our headteacher, Mrs Li, always looked at the displays at parents' evening. Sometimes she even gave congratulations and recognitions during the morning announcements if something impressed her.

I could already imagine her voice: *I'd like*

to recognize and congratulate Azaleah Lane for her fantastic model.

Before we left the zoo, Miss Johnson let us go to the gift shop. I only had enough money for one postcard. I could look at the panda cam any time, so I decided to get one of Nikita the tiger.

I spent the whole walk back to school chatting with Rose and trying to choose an animal for my model. Whatever I made for Monday was going to impress Mrs Li, I would make sure of it.

CHAPTER 2

GUESS WHAT?

After school I ran straight to Mum's car. I couldn't wait to tell her about our school trip. And now I had the chance to earn extra science points. That was almost as exciting as the zoo.

My little sister, Tiana, was in her car seat in the back. When I opened the door she yelled, "Hi, Azaleah! Guess what? Auntie Sam took me and Kevin to the park today!"

I smiled at Tiana. Auntie Sam was my mum's younger sister. She babysat us all the time. We always did fun things with her.

"I got to go to the zoo today," I told Tiana.

"It was awesome!"

Mum laughed. "Sounds like everyone
had a good day."

"That's not all!" I shouted. "I get to make
a model habitat this weekend for extra science
points."

"Azaleah, strap in so we can go and pick
up Nia from school," said Mum. "I need to get
to work to prepare for the dinner rush."

I fastened my seat belt. Mum always
worked on Friday nights. Her restaurant, Avec
Amour, was jam-packed at weekends. On
Fridays, she had musicians performing. People
loved Mum's cooking, and Avec Amour had
won a "Favourite Local Restaurant" prize.
Even famous people ate there!

Usually Friday nights were Daddy nights.
He would meet us at the restaurant after
school and take us home so that Mum
could work. Sometimes we got to eat at the

restaurant and listen to the music for a little while before we left.

Tonight wasn't going to be a Daddy night, though. He'd told us at breakfast that he had to work late tonight too.

Dad is a very good lawyer. Everybody says so. He was working on a big case, helping some sick people sue a big medicine company. The medicine had made people more poorly instead of better. My dad was trying to make the company pay the sick people money.

"Mum, which do you like better? Pandas or tigers?" I asked.

Before Mum could answer, Tiana chimed in. "Today me and Kevin dug a great big hole in the ground," she said.

"Kevin and *I*," I corrected. "And stop interrupting!"

"I like them both," said Mum. I was glad she'd ignored Tiana.

A few minutes later, we pulled up to my big sister Nia's school. Nia was already outside waiting. She was smiling and waving her arms around while she talked to some other girls. As soon as she saw us, she ran to the car.

Nia jumped into the front seat and threw her bag on the floor. Her eyes looked like they were about to pop right out of her head.

"Guess what?" she said. "I got the lead part! I get to be Dorothy in *The Wizard of Oz*!" She held up a plastic bag. "Mr. Guidi has already given me my costume!"

"Oh, Nia!" cried Mum. She leaned across the seat and gave Nia a big hug.

"Bravo!" I clapped for Nia. Tiana quickly copied me.

I was proud of Nia. For the past two weeks she had been preparing to audition for the musical. I knew she wanted to be Dorothy more than anything. Nia worked hard. She deserved to be the main character.

"Nia, today I slid backwards down the slide," said Tiana.

I asked, "Should I make a model about the pandas or something else?"

"I'm definitely going to be famous one day," said Nia.

Mum shook her head. "So much excitement!"

When we got to Avec Amour, Auntie Sam was already there waiting for us. "How are my favourite nieces?" she asked.

Nia laughed. Auntie Sam always said that when she picked us up.

"We're your only nieces," Nia pointed out, as always.

"Thanks for picking them up, Sam," said Mum. She kissed all four of us goodbye and rushed back to the kitchen.

We had to walk quite a long way to get to
Auntie Sam's car. Avec Amour was on a busy
street with lots of shops and restaurants but
not many parking spaces.

"There's too much traffic in this part of
town," said Auntie Sam. She always said that
too.

We finally got to her car, but the drive

home took forever. Finally we got closer to our nice, quiet neighbourhood.

Auntie Sam sighed. "I love your road." She always said that too.

Our neighbourhood was all houses, so the only people who drove around in it were the ones who lived there. Ours was huge and

white, so I called it the White House.

Auntie Sam parked in the driveway. As we walked into the house, she asked, "What do you guys want to do tonight?"

"Play!" shouted Tiana.

"Model!" I shouted. I ran to my room to get started.

My room was the best one in the house. Auntie Sam had painted it light green with one lavender wall. Dad had filled my bookshelf with science books, gemstones and a microscope. Mum had created an art corner next to my bed complete with glitter and paint and clay and glue.

And my room always smelled good, because Mum made me sachets. They were little pouches filled with things like cinnamon or lavender or rosemary.

I heard Nia running to her room on the third floor. I knew she was about to rehearse in front of the mirror, as usual. Nia could dance and sing and act. Dad called her a triple threat.

Maybe she really will be famous one day, I thought.

I reached under my bed to pull out a shoebox. I needed it for my model.

"Azaleah?"

I recognized Tiana's voice without looking. Tiana was an interrupter. "*Yes?*" I said.

Tiana stood in front of me and frowned. "Did you take Greenie?" she asked.

"No," I said. Greenie was Tiana's favourite stuffed animal. She took him almost everywhere.

"Are you sure?" she asked.

"I wouldn't take Greenie," I said. I didn't think *anyone* would take Greenie. He was a speckled frog with bulging eyes, and he was *very* dirty.

Tiana's eyes got so big she looked like Greenie. "Then guess what? Somebody *stealed* him!"

"Nobody *stole* him," I corrected her.

Tiana nodded her head really fast. "Uh-huh," she said. "Somebody did! He was here earlier. And now he's gone!"

CHAPTER 3
THE SEARCH FOR GREENIE

Tears rolled down Tiana's cheeks. I knew she wasn't messing around. Greenie really was missing. And that meant one thing – we had a mystery on our hands.

I wanted to start my model. I had already decided to make a tiger habitat. Everyone in my class loved the giant pandas, but that meant everyone would probably be making a panda habitat. I wanted mine to be unique.

Plus, Nikita was really interesting. Even though she was a big tiger with sharp teeth and claws, the zookeeper said she was still a little bit scared in her new home.

But I also loved a challenge. Greenie's disappearance was a mystery. And a mystery was definitely a challenge. I was an excellent mystery solver too. One time I found Mum's missing keys. Another time I found Dad's glasses.

Plus I knew Tiana wouldn't leave me alone if I didn't help her.

"OK, think, Tiana," I said. "When was the last time you had Greenie?"

"I told you, I had him earlier," she said. "But now he's gone."

I knew what that meant. It meant she'd taken him somewhere and forgotten where she left him.

"Maybe he's in the living room," I said. "You probably left him in there while you were playing."

Tiana shook her head. "No, I didn't."

I went to the living room anyway. I looked behind the sofa, under the pillows and in the toy box. No Greenie.

"Maybe you left him in the kitchen at snack time," I suggested.

Tiana didn't look like she believed me, but she followed me anyway. We searched every cupboard and drawer in the kitchen. We found appliances, seasonings, pots and pans, and food-storage containers. But no Greenie.

Greenie is more lost than I expected, I thought.

I went out the back door and found Auntie Sam sitting on a sun lounger. She loved to sit in our garden. We had a patio, grass, bushes and lots of flowers. Auntie Sam didn't have a garden at her house.

"Auntie Sam?" I said. "Have you seen Greenie?"

Auntie Sam looked up from the home-design magazine she was reading. She was an interior design – that meant it was her job to design the inside of people's houses. Her dog, Woofer, looked up at me too.

Auntie Sam thought for a minute. "Tiana had him at the park," she finally said.

Tiana was standing behind me. "But I brought him home for his nap."

This mystery was turning out to be what Mum called "time consuming". That meant it was taking too long. I had a model to make!

I looked at Tiana. Her bottom lip was poking out. I knew if I stopped searching she would start crying.

Auntie Sam spread her arms, and Tiana climbed onto the chair for a hug.

"He's here somewhere," Auntie Sam promised. "Why don't you pretend you're hunting for treasure?"

"Let's look in the bathroom," I suggested.

"He's not there," said Tiana. "He's not even potty trained."

I went to the bathroom anyway. "Maybe you took him with you when *you* went," I said.

In the bathroom, I looked in the bath and in the cabinets. I looked everywhere. But Tiana was right. Greenie wasn't there.

We spent more than an hour searching. We checked Mum's room, Dad's office and the hall cupboard.

"Maybe Greenie is somewhere in *your* room," I told Tiana.

Tiana's bottom lip quivered and her eyes filled with tears. "He's not! I looked in my wardrobe and my bed and under it too. I looked on my shelf and took everything out of my toy box."

I sighed. Those were all of the places I would have looked.

There was only one place left to search: Nia's room.

I did *not* want to check Nia's room. Nia was never as patient about interruptions as I was. Interruptions made Nia grumpy. But I knew that if I ever wanted to start my model, we had to check her room.

Tiana and I went upstairs. Nia's door was shut. She was singing – *loudly.* I was glad she had a good voice because otherwise my eardrums would probably crack.

"Knock on the door," I whispered to Tiana.

Tiana shook her head. "You knock."

"Just knock," I said.

Tiana shook her head again.

I sighed and knocked on the door. I didn't have time to argue.

"What?" Nia yelled. "I'm rehearsing!"

"We need help," I replied through the closed door.

Nia swung open her door and stood there with one hand on her hip. She had picked her hair into an Afro and was wearing her costume. The button-up top, skirt and white

earrings made her look just like Dorothy.
She also had on lipstick and was holding a
little stuffed dog.

I peeked into her room to see what else
was going on in there.

"Don't be nosy," said Nia. She shut her
door a little bit.

I frowned. I didn't like being called nosy.
I was just curious.

"What do you two want?" asked Nia
again.

"Did you take Greenie?" I asked.

Nia rolled her eyes. "*Greenie?* Why would
I take Greenie?"

"Greenie is GONE!" Tiana cried.

"Well," said Nia, "he's not in here. I don't
steal. I don't have time to steal anyway. I'm
busy."

With that, she closed the door and
started singing again. I could hear her feet

stomping on the floor, so I knew she was dancing too.

A tear rolled down Tiana's cheek. "Where is he?" she asked.

I thought about my empty shoebox. This day was turning out to be *too* challenging.

"Could you have left Greenie somewhere while you were out with Auntie Sam?" I asked.

"No! I didn't leave him anywhere," Tiana insisted.

While I stood there thinking, Auntie Sam called, "Girls! Dinner!"

I ran to the kitchen to see what Mum had left for us to eat. Tiana followed me. In the kitchen, Auntie Sam was dishing up red beans and rice, pork chops and green vegetables.

"I have to find Greenie!" Tiana whined.

Nia skipped into the kitchen, still wearing her costume. "I don't have time to eat," she said. "I need to rehearse."

"No arguing," Auntie Sam said firmly. "We're eating together. Sit down."

* * *

After dinner, we all searched high and low. I looked in the washing machine and the tumble dryer. Auntie Sam checked the kitchen drawers and cupboards again. Tiana looked in the fridge and the wardrobes.

Nia offered to look in her room. I knew Greenie wasn't in there. Nia just wanted to rehearse.

By the time Mum and Dad got home, Nia wasn't the only one putting on a show. Tiana was sulking. Auntie Sam was blasting Dad's Earth, Wind & Fire record, trying to cheer Tiana up.

I was starting to get frustrated. I hadn't even *started* my model.

"Why are you girls still awake?" Dad asked us.

"We have a problem," said Auntie Sam. "Greenie is missing."

Mum picked up Tiana. Dad turned off the music.

"It's time for bed," he said.

Nobody argued with Dad.

We quickly brushed our teeth and got into bed. But down the hall, I could hear Tiana in her room, crying.

I tiptoed to her room and peeked through her doorway. "I'll help you look more tomorrow," I whispered. "I promise."

Tiana nodded, and I snuck back to my bed. I stared at the heart-shaped shadows my night light made on the walls. I needed to solve this mystery so I could start my model in the morning. If I wanted it to impress Mrs Li, it had to be perfect.

CHAPTER 4
NO PEACE

My eyes popped open bright and early the next morning. I knew straight away what day it was: Saturday.

I loved Saturdays. Our family called them Lazy Saturdays. Dad and I were the early birds. We always got up first. Mum slept in because she worked late on Fridays. Nia and Tiana usually slept late too.

But this Saturday was going to be less lazy than usual. I had a tiger habitat to make! I made my plan before I got out of bed.

1. Eat cereal with Dad, as always.
2. Watch *one* cartoon instead of three.
3. Paint the inside of my shoebox before everyone else wakes up.
4. Work on my tiger while the paint dries.

I crept to my door extra quietly, so Tiana wouldn't wake up. I knew she would want to search for Greenie. That would ruin my morning plan.

But when I opened my door, I saw I had a big problem. Tiana was asleep on the floor.

She was curled up, just like a cat, with her pillow and a blanket.

I tried to sneak past. But as soon as I stepped my first foot over, Tiana woke up.

"Hi, Azaleah!" she said. "Ready?"

I knew what she meant, but I said, "Ready for what?"

"To find Greenie," she said. "You promised."

I always kept my promises, but I had to *stall*. I was not ready, because I already had a plan. And I hadn't even got to step one of it yet.

I had to think fast. Maybe I could add Tiana to steps one and two. Then I could sneak away while she watched cartoons.

"Let's go and eat and watch cartoons first," I suggested. "Then we can look for Greenie."

Tiana shook her head. "I want to look for Greenie now."

I remembered what Mum always said: "Food feeds the body and the soul." I just had to convince Tiana.

"If we eat first, we'll have lots of energy," I said. "Then we can find Greenie faster."

"Faster?" asked Tiana.

I nodded.

"OK," said Tiana.

We went to the kitchen. I expected to see Dad at the table. He always drank his coffee and worked on his laptop until I got up.

But when I walked into the kitchen, I knew something was wrong. Dad wasn't wearing the black dressing gown and matching slippers he always wore on Saturdays. He was wearing work clothes. His work bag was on the table. And he was pouring coffee into the mug he took to his office.

"Dad? What are you doing?" I asked.

Dad kissed me. Then he looked at Tiana and said, "Hey, pip-squeak." He gave her a kiss too.

"Are you leaving?" I asked.

Dad nodded. "Yeah. No cartoons for me today. I have to work on this case."

"Oh," I said. I felt bad for Dad, but I also felt bad for myself. My plan was getting really messed up.

Dad got the cereal from the cupboard and handed it to me. Then he headed out the door.

As soon as he left, Tiana started to whine. She didn't want cereal. She'd changed her mind about cartoons. All she wanted was Greenie.

I ate my cereal and walked to the living room to turn on the TV. I was determined to finish step two of my plan.

Mum and Nia were up now too. Mum was holding some paper, and Nia was standing in front of the TV. I realized that they were going over Nia's lines. Mum had the script. If Nia forgot what to say, Mum would help her.

"Can I watch TV?" I asked.

Just then Tiana walked in, climbed on to Mum's lap, and said, "Can you help me find Greenie?"

"I'm trying to rehearse!" yelled Nia.

Mum said, "Nia, calm down. Azaleah, go and help Tiana look for Greenie while we practise. Then when we're done, you can watch TV."

Nia stuck her tongue out at me. Tiana clapped. Mum smiled.

I didn't have anything nice to say, so I decided not to say anything at all. Instead I fast-walked down the hall with Tiana right behind me. I sat on my bed. Saturday was already ruined.

"Where else could Greenie be?" Tiana asked.

I shrugged. I was out of ideas. We had already looked all over the house. Then it hit me: *Maybe Greenie isn't in the house.*

"Tell me every single thing you did yesterday," I said. "Start at the beginning."

Tiana grinned. "First Auntie Sam let me and Kevin play at the park for a long time.

Then we walked to the postbox. Then we walked to Kevin's house." She took a breath. "Then we saw Mr Givens in his garden. Then it was nap time."

I sighed. *Great,* I thought. *Greenie could be anywhere. This is going to take all day.*

CHAPTER 5

WILD GOOSE CHASE

I went back to the living room with Tiana right behind me. "Mum," I said, "Greenie might be somewhere outside."

Mum put Nia's script on the table. "Nia," she said, "can you take your sisters out to retrace Tiana's steps?"

Nia groaned. "But, Mum, I need to practise."

Mum gave her a look. "Nia, I was at the restaurant late last night, and I have to go back in a few hours to prep for dinner. I really need some rest. And I need to plan the daily specials for the week."

Tiana started to cry again. *"Please,* Nia? I miss Greenie. He's my best friend."

Nia bent down and wiped Tiana's tears. "I have an idea," she said. "Why don't I practise my lines while we search? I'll be Dorothy looking for home, and you can be Tiana looking for Greenie."

Tiana gave Nia a great big hug, but all I could think was, *I wish I could make a model while we search.*

After we got dressed, Nia took us outside. She looked around at our neighbourhood like she'd never seen it before. I had a feeling she was pretending to have landed in Oz, just like Dorothy.

"Where should we start?" Nia asked.

Since Tiana had gone to the park first yesterday, we decided to start there. At least it was close, and it was fun to look at our neighbours' gardens.

When we got to the park, we walked down a path to get to the play area. A lady in a sun hat was pulling up weeds in the park garden. A man and a woman were having a picnic on the grass.

Nia wandered around singing while Tiana and I looked all over. I even climbed around on the climbing frames looking for Greenie.

Finally I shook my head. Greenie wasn't

at the park.

Nia stood up. "Let's go to the Emerald City next."

I giggled. Emerald City was a place in *The Wizard of Oz*. "We haven't found Greenie yet," I said. I knew Tiana wouldn't let us rest until we did. "Let's check the postbox next."

Tiana said, "I told you I brought him home. Somebody *stealed* him."

"Stole," I corrected her.

We crossed the street and walked to the corner where the postbox was. I got on my hands and knees and looked behind it. No Greenie.

"Maybe you posted him," Nia joked.

Tiana started to cry. "I didn't. I brought him home."

I could tell Nia felt bad about making Tiana cry. "I was just kidding, Tiana," she said. She went back to her Dorothy voice.

"Maybe the Wizard will help us."

While Nia was busy being Dorothy, I remembered Tiana saying that Auntie Sam took Kevin home after they went to the postbox.

"Let's go to Kevin's house," I suggested. "It's on the way home."

"Greenie's not there!" Tiana yelled. "I brought him home!"

"Let's just make sure," I said.

We walked to Kevin's house and knocked on the front door. Kevin's mum answered.

A minute later, Kevin came running through. He had on pyjamas with trains all over them.

"Hi, Tiana! Wanna play?" he asked.

Tiana shook her head. "I can't find Greenie."

"You took him home," Kevin said.

We all stood there looking at each other. I knew there had to be another answer. There had to be something Tiana was forgetting.

Greenie was *not* at home.

Kevin's mum looked at him. "Are you sure?" she said.

"Uh-huh," said Kevin. "He waved goodbye to me when he left."

Tiana smiled. "He likes you, Kevin."

We left Kevin's house and headed back to the White House. Mr Givens, our next-door neighbour, was outside digging a hole. He was outside a lot. Mr Givens lived on his own but he didn't seem sad about it. He smiled all the time, and he always had treats.

As soon as he saw us, Mr Givens said, "Well, if it isn't the Lane girls. My favourite neighbours."

"Hi, Mr Givens," I replied. "What are you doing?"

"Today I'm planting a cookie tree." He winked at us.

Tiana giggled. "Cookies don't grow on trees!"

"We'll see," said Mr Givens. "Wait right here." He disappeared inside and came back out with a paper bag. He reached in and handed us two chocolate chip cookies each. "These are fresh," he said. "Just off the tree."

"Thank you," I said, taking a bite. "Have you seen a green stuffed frog?"

Mr Givens smiled. "You mean Greenie? I sure did."

"Where?" I asked.

"I saw him yesterday right here. He waved to me," said Mr Givens.

Tiana had a cookie in her mouth, but that didn't stop her from talking. "He likes you," she said. Cookie crumbs dropped out of her mouth and landed on the ground.

"I like him too." Mr Givens started digging his hole again.

This mystery was starting to get complicated. It was like Greenie had disappeared into thin air.

"Tiana," I said. "You're forgetting *something*. Where else could Greenie be?"

Tiana started to cry again. "Nowhere. I brought him home. I tucked him in for his nap. Then he was gone."

"Wait a minute." I stopped and stared at my little sister. "You tucked him in? You mean you know *exactly* where you put Greenie?"

I looked at Nia. Her mouth dropped open. We had just walked all over the place for nothing. I realized I should have asked Tiana more questions. Better questions. I should have asked exactly *where* she'd had Greenie. I had only asked *when* she had him.

Tiana had a proud look on her face. "It was nap time," she said. "I told you."

It was true. She *had* told me. She'd just left out some details – important details. And I hadn't believed her. I'd never even investigated Tiana's room. I'd been so worried about hurrying up that I had actually *wasted* time.

CHAPTER 6
CALM ON THE OUTSIDE

When we got back home, Mum was at her desk in the kitchen. "Did you find Greenie?" she asked.

Before Tiana could answer, Nia said, "No." She frowned. "I stopped rehearsing for nothing."

I could tell Nia was about to act *dramatic*. I think Mum could tell too, because she said, "Don't start, Nia."

Tiana started to cry. "Mum, what if I never ever see Greenie again?"

"We'll find him," Mum promised.

Nia plopped down in a chair with her script. She read her lines *very* loudly. Tiana sat in Mum's lap. Tears dripped onto Mum's paper.

I watched Tiana and Mum and thought about two things: Greenie and my model. They were both important, but I needed to pick one.

"Mum?" I said. "Can I go and work on my model?"

"No!" Tiana yelled. "We have to find Greenie! You promised!"

I took three calming breaths, just like Miss Johnson made us do in class when everyone got too loud after break. This mystery was a challenge *and* a problem.

Tiana had already messed up my plan for the day. She had already messed up Nia's rehearsal. She was probably messing up Mum's morning too. Mum loved lazy Saturdays.

Mum said, "Tiana, let's take a little break and look more later."

I was relieved. "Can I go and work on my model, please?" I asked.

Tiana frowned, then tilted her head back and let out a long cry. She reminded me of the baby elephant I'd seen at the zoo, only Tiana didn't have a trunk. Between her and Nia, our kitchen sounded like a *zoo*.

Mum looked like *she* needed to take three calming breaths. She put down her pencil and looked at Nia.

"Nia, why don't you see if you can rehearse at Maya's house?" she said. "Isn't she playing Auntie Em?"

Nia smiled and nodded. Her best friend, Maya, lived near us. "I'll text her," she said.

She grabbed her phone, her script and her

costume. A few minutes later, Nia hurried out the door.

Next, Mum stood Tiana on the floor. She crouched down and put her face very close to Tiana's face.

"That's enough," she said. "Nap time. Right now."

Tiana opened her mouth, but before she could make another sound, Mum said, "*Now.*"

Mum meant business. Tiana sulked out of the kitchen.

Once the kitchen was quiet, Mum hugged me. "Why don't I make us some lunch?" she offered.

I perked right up. I almost never got Mum all to myself. I helped her make roast beef sandwiches on toasted sourdough rolls. Then we sat down to eat.

"So, what have you done so far on your

model?" Mum asked.

"Nothing," I said. "All I have so far is an empty box."

She smiled. "I have an idea."

Mum stood up and took a piece of paper and a pencil from a drawer. "The best thing to do when you have a lot to get done is make a list," she explained.

She handed the paper to me. "Why don't you start by writing down the steps for your model?"

"Is that what you do at the restaurant?" I asked.

Mum nodded and grabbed her daily special planner too. "We'll both make our to-do lists," she said. She sat down, opened the planner and got started on it straight away.

I took the pencil and thought for a minute. Then I got to work too.

1. Paint box blue and green.

2. Make clay tiger.

3. Make paper grass.

4. Collect plants from outside.

5. Paint tiger.

6. Stick everything on the scene.

I looked at what I'd written. I'd thought making a list would help, but it made me feel worse. There were six steps, and I had less than two days. I might not finish my model in time.

Just then, Dad came home. He kissed Mum first, then me.

"Looks like you two are having a nice, calm, lazy Saturday," he said.

I thought about my walking all over the neighbourhood for nothing. I thought about Nia's loud rehearsing. I thought about Tiana's crying. Then I thought about my unfinished model and the unsolved mystery.

Maybe I *looked* calm, but that was only on the outside.

CHAPTER 7

MODEL DISASTER

Dad sat down at the kitchen table and took a sandwich off the plate Mum had put on the table. He took a great big bite. "Mmmmm," he said.

Mum giggled and stood up. "I'd better get to work," she said. "I'm so glad I took tomorrow off." Then she grabbed her planner and her chef uniform and left.

I let out a sigh. I'd been hoping for Mum's help.

Once we were alone, Dad turned to me. "What's up?"

This was the first chance I'd had to talk to Dad about the zoo and my extra science point homework. First, I told him all about my school trip. Then, I said, "Now I get to make a model. I'm making a tiger habitat."

"Wow!" said Dad. "Can I see it?"

"There's nothing to see," I said.

I updated Dad on our not-so-lazy Saturday, and about Greenie. He listened to every single word I said. That was my favourite thing about Dad. He was a very good listener.

"Well, I guess you'd better get to it," he said. "The house is nice and quiet now."

I went to my room and put my list on my desk. Then I pulled out the art mat Auntie Sam had bought me for my birthday. The mat helped keep my desk clean.

Next, I got out blue and green paint, a paint brush and my clay. Then, I put my apron on over my clothes so they wouldn't get dirty. Auntie Sam had given it to me with the mat.

Finally I sat down at my desk. I was ready. First, I painted half of the box blue. That would be the sky.

Then, I painted the other half green. That would be the grass. I didn't want the outside of the box to look like a shoebox, so I painted the whole outside black.

Finishing that step made me feel better. I put the box to the side to dry. I crossed step one off my list. Step two was going to be the most fun: making the clay tiger.

I pulled out the postcard I'd bought at the zoo's gift shop. It had a picture of Nikita on the front. I was really glad that I'd bought it before we left.

I started to shape the clay. It wasn't as easy as I thought it would be. At first it looked like

a rock with legs. Then, it looked like a dog.
Finally it was just right.

Just then, Tiana came crashing into my
room. She didn't even knock.

"Let's look for Greenie!" she shouted,
barrelling towards me.

Before I could even put my tiger aside, Tiana bumped my desk and knocked Nikita onto the floor. When I picked her up, Nikita was *ruined*. One side of my tiger was squashed flat. Two legs and one ear had come off. Every single little whisker I'd made had fallen off too.

"Look what you did!" I shouted. I stood up, grabbed Tiana's hand, and pulled her to the door. "Get out!"

Tiana did her baby-elephant cry again.
"Owwwwww," she whined.

"Get out!" I yelled. "You broke my tiger!"

I pulled Tiana all the way out of my room.
Unfortunately, I ran right into Dad.
I quickly let go of Tiana's arm.

Dad looked at us. He had a pencil behind
his ear and was wearing his glasses.
I knew he had been in his office working.
Tiana and Greenie were interrupting
everyone's day.

At first I thought I was going to have some
explaining to do. But Dad walked right past
me. He went into my room and picked up the
tiger pieces. He stared at them for a minute.
Then he put them on the desk and walked
over to Tiana.

Dad bent down so his face was very close
to Tiana's face. "What do you need to say to
your sister?" he asked.

Tiana frowned. "But, Dad, I only wanted –"

"I don't want to hear it," Dad said firmly.

I was glad to have Dad on my side. My model was just as important as Greenie. Tiana had a whole toy box full of stuffed toys.

Dad repeated his question: "What do you need to say to Azaleah?"

"I'm sorry I broke your tiger," Tiana mumbled.

I nodded, but I did *not* forgive her. Not for one second. Nikita was ruined. She needed a *vet*.

So much for step two, I thought.

Dad said, "Azaleah, see if you can fix your project." Then he led Tiana away and shut my door. Even though the door was closed, I heard him tell Tiana not to interrupt me again.

I sighed. Sometimes having a baby sister was very annoying.

* * *

By the time I finished fixing my tiger, it was time for dinner. At the weekend, we usually had leftovers from Avec Amour, as Mum needed to be at the restaurant.

Dad heated up the food and put it on the table. Today Mum had left us macaroni cheese and glazed ham. She'd also left some homemade rolls.

A few minutes later, Nia walked back in from her rehearsal. She was dressed up in her Dorothy costume, and she had on very long fake eyelashes. Her Afro was nice and round.

The whole time we ate, Nia pretended to be Dorothy. If anyone talked to her, she gave an answer that didn't even make any sense.

Dad asked, "Nia, how was your rehearsal?"

"I'm on my way to find the Wizard," said Nia. "I have to find my way back home." She bent down and picked up the stuffed Toto from the floor. She hugged him and stared into space.

Dad laughed, but Toto must have reminded Tiana of Greenie. She started crying again. "I want Greenie!" she wailed.

"Ugh, Tiana!" said Nia. "Give it a rest. Nobody wants to hear any more about Greenie."

Of course, that made Tiana cry more. I wished Tiana could go spend the night at Auntie Sam's this weekend. Maybe she could stay at Kevin's house. I didn't care where she went. It was worth a try.

"I think a sleepover might cheer Tiana up," I suggested.

Tiana stopped crying and grinned.

"Maybe I can have a sleepover with *you*!" she said.

I shook my head. I did not want to spend one more minute with my little sister, even if I did have a mystery to solve. I needed to do three steps today and three steps tomorrow if I wanted to finish my model. Thanks to Tiana, I had already spent way too much time on step two. I had to get step three done before bed.

"No way," I said.

Tiana went back to crying.

Lazy Saturday had quickly turned into crazy Saturday. Dad wiped his mouth and scraped his chair back from the table.

"Everyone is going to bed," he said. "Now."

I started to cry. I tried not to, but I couldn't help it. I couldn't go to bed. I had to make my paper grass.

"Dad," said Nia. "It's six o'clock."

"I don't care," Dad said. "This is ridiculous."

Nia stomped upstairs with Toto. I looked at Tiana. This was all her fault. She didn't even look like she felt sorry. She was smiling.

"Dad," she said, "can I have a sleepover with Azaleah?"

"You have caused enough trouble for one day," Dad said.

Tiana gave Dad her sweetest smile. "Pleeeeeeeaaaase?" she begged.

Dad thought for a long time. Finally he looked at me and winked. I knew what that meant: he had a plan.

"If I let you have a sleepover in Azaleah's room, do you promise not to bother her tomorrow?" he asked Tiana.

I smiled at him. Dad was clever. We had to go to bed either way. If Tiana agreed and came with me, I'd have all day tomorrow to finish my model.

Tiana grinned and nodded. "Yes, Dad. I promise."

Finally, I'll have some peace, I thought. *And tomorrow, I'll have an awesome model.*

CHAPTER 8

WORST SLEEPOVER EVER

Slumber parties should be fun. They should be with your best friends. But as soon as my slumber party with Tiana started, I knew it wasn't going to be either of those things.

Tiana dragged her sleeping bag and pillow into my room. She spread her stuff out right next to my bed and snuggled up with a big smile on her face.

My little sister obviously thought she'd won. But I knew *I* was the winner.

When Dad came to tuck us in, he said, "Go straight to sleep. No messing around in here." He kissed us and shut the door.

"Will you sleep on the floor with me?" asked Tiana.

I thought about Dad's deal. If a good sleepover kept Tiana away from me tomorrow, it was worth it.

"OK," I agreed. "But don't forget – tomorrow you leave me alone." I pulled my covers onto the floor and made a bed next to Tiana.

First, Tiana talked. I ignored her. Then, she sang herself a lullaby.

"Shhhhh!" I whisper-shouted.

Tiana stopped singing and hummed very softly. Eventually my eyes closed. But as soon as I fell asleep, Tiana woke me up with her crying.

"What's wrong?" I asked.

"I miss Greenie," she whispered. "What if he's scared without me?"

"Frogs can be nocturnal," I said. I'd learnt that at the zoo. "Greenie is probably fine."

Tiana sniffled. "How do you know he'll be fine? What's nocturnal?"

"That means he likes to be awake at night. You're *not* nocturnal. You'll feel better if you go to sleep," I said.

I turned over and thought about which plants I needed to collect for my model. Next to me, Tiana finally fell asleep. I could tell because she started snoring very softly. It was cute.

What was *not* cute was when I woke up in the middle of the night with Tiana sleeping on top of me. She had wiggled all the way onto my covers and was lying on my arm.

My arm had fallen asleep too and was tingling. I couldn't even move because I didn't want to wake Tiana up. I knew if I did she'd start whining about Greenie again.

Finally Tiana did move. She started tossing and turning in her sleep, almost like she was running. She mumbled Greenie's name.

Tiana ran and mumbled for a long time. When she was done, she had turned herself all the way around. Now her toes were touching my cheek.

I had no choice. I had to wake her up.

"Tiana, move," I whispered. I pushed her feet out of my face.

Tiana sat up and looked around like she had forgotten where she was. When she saw me, she turned around and put her head on my pillow. I hoped she would go back to sleep, but . . .

"I want Greenie," she whispered.

"I want Greenie too," I muttered.

Tiana said, "Where do you think he went?"

I was having a hard time with this mystery. I didn't know where Greenie could be. But if I told Tiana that, she would start crying again.

Suddenly I remembered something Miss Johnson had taught us: *the process of elimination.* She said when you didn't know an answer, you should think about what the answer was *not.* Greenie was *not* in the neighbourhood or in the house. But Tiana knew where she'd left him. That was the confusing part.

I knew what I had to do. We had to return to the scene of the crime.

"Tiana," I whispered. "I need you to show me where Greenie was."

Tiana got excited. "Right now?"

"Shhhhh," I whispered. Looking for clues might also get us in trouble. If Dad caught us out of bed, he'd be cross. "Yes, right now. But you have to be really quiet."

I opened my door and peeked down the landing. The house was dark except for the night-light in the bathroom.

We tiptoed past Mum and Dad's room. Their door was open a tiny bit, and they were asleep.

We got to the end of the landing without making a single peep. When we reached

Tiana's room, I quietly shut the door behind us. Then I sat on Tiana's bed.

"OK, where was Greenie?" I asked.

"He was *right there*," she said.

"Right where?" I asked.

"There," Tiana said. She pointed to the corner of her room near the night-light. There was a small doll bed on the floor, right next to Tiana's purple boots.

"In the doll bed?" I asked.

Tiana nodded.

"Tell me the whole story," I said. I got ready to listen very carefully.

"It was nap time," said Tiana. "I tucked in Miss Betty first. Then I tucked in Puff Puff. Then I tucked in Greenie. I gave them kisses, and I got into bed. I had a nap."

I looked at the doll bed. Miss Betty, Tiana's doll with curly hair, was still there. So was Puff Puff the Kitty. "Then what?" I asked.

Tiana looked at me. "Then nothing. I was asleep."

"What did you do when you woke up?" I asked.

"Mum woke me up. Auntie Sam and Woofer were gone. Mum made me hurry because we had to go and get you." Tiana frowned. "She picked me up straight out of the bed and carried me to the car."

It didn't make any sense at all. "Did you take Greenie?" I asked.

"Mum wouldn't let me." Tiana's frown got bigger. "I didn't remember him till I was buckled in my car seat. She said we were late."

"Hmm," I said. "Was Greenie still in bed when you left?"

Tiana tilted her head to one side. "I don't know. I didn't look."

I looked at the doll bed again. I crouched down on the floor. I stared at Miss Betty. The

blanket was pulled up to her chin. Puff Puff was right next to her.

Then I looked at the spot where Greenie was supposed to be. The blanket had been moved just a little bit. One corner of it had a smudge on it. It looked like chocolate.

I sniffed it, but the smudge didn't smell like chocolate. It smelt like soil. There were also a couple of tiny leaves on the floor next to the doll bed.

Something was not quite right. But I didn't know what it was.

Before I could think of a hypothesis about Greenie, Tiana's door opened. Tiana and I both jumped.

Dad stood there frowning at us. "Back to bed," he said. "NOW."

We did what he said. He stood on the landing and watched us go back to my room. Tiana and I got under my covers together.

My brain was busy trying to figure out the clues I'd found.

"Tiana, were your feet dirty when you got home?" I whispered.

"I don't know," she whispered back.

I needed to go back to the scene of the crime first thing tomorrow morning. I also needed to work on my model, but I was determined to crack this case. I had a feeling I was getting close.

CHAPTER 9

UNUSUAL SUSPECT

Early the next morning, Tiana tapped my forehead with her finger. "Can we look for Greenie?" she asked.

I got up straight away. The clue about the soil might help me solve the mystery. Then I would have the rest of the day to work on my model.

Tiana and I ran to her room. Now that it was morning, we didn't have to sneak. I knelt on the floor next to the doll bed. Puff Puff and Miss Betty were still sleeping. They were right where we'd left them.

So was the dirty spot. So was the leaf.

"Do you remember what shoes you had on?" I asked. Maybe Tiana had left the dirty spot.

Tiana went to the wardrobe to get her trainers. She handed them to me, and I turned them upside down. The bottoms were clean.

I pointed to the soil and leaf. "Look," I said. "How did that get there?"

Tiana got on the floor next to me. She looked at the spot and crossed her arms. "Somebody made my doll bed dirty!" she said. "And *stealed* Greenie. I told you."

What kind of thief would come in and steal a stuffed animal? I thought. Nothing else was missing. It didn't make sense. I needed more information.

"Did you hear anything while you were napping?" I asked.

Tiana laughed at me. "No, silly. You can't hear while you're asleep."

I took three deep breaths. "Did anything wake you up?"

"Just Mum," she said.

"Did you hear anything *before* you fell asleep?" I asked.

Tiana tilted her head to the side again. She stayed like that for a while. "Yes!" she said. "I heard jingle bells."

"'Jingle Bells'?" I asked. "Like the song?"

"Like the bells," Tiana said. "Like the kind on an elf's hat."

That didn't help at all. Tiana had probably been dreaming. An elf had definitely *not* stolen Greenie.

While I was trying to think, the doorbell rang. Tiana and I ran downstairs. When we got to the front door, Mum was giving Auntie Sam a hug. Woofer was running around them.

Auntie Sam saw us and grinned. "Hi! What are you girls up to?" she asked.

Mum went back to the kitchen to finish cooking. Sometimes she left someone else in charge of breakfast at the restaurant on Sundays. Whenever she took a Sunday off, she made brunch. And Auntie Sam always came over.

"I'm solving a mystery," I said. "We still can't find Greenie."

"Still?" Auntie Sam said.

Tiana yelled, "Somebody *stealed* him!"

Auntie Sam raised one eyebrow. "Greenie was stolen?"

Tiana and I both nodded. Then I told Auntie Sam about the soil and leaf I'd discovered in Tiana's room.

A few minutes later, Mum yelled, "Breakfast is ready!"

Everyone hurried to the kitchen. Nia came downstairs, singing a song. She sounded *really* good. Auntie Sam knew the song too, so she started singing along. Then Dad came in and sang with them.

Mum laughed and said, "Sit down and eat, everyone."

The table was full of food. Mum had made bacon, eggs, hash browns, fruit, croissants and orange juice. Woofer put his nose up to the table, and Auntie Sam shooed him away.

We all ate and talked. For a little while I forgot all about Greenie *and* my model.

When everyone stood up to help clear the table, Woofer came running through the kitchen. He had Dad's slipper in his mouth.

Dad yelled, "Catch that thief!"

"Don't let him take that outside!" Auntie Sam exclaimed. "He'll bury it, and you'll never see it again."

Suddenly I realized the slipper wasn't just a slipper – it was a *clue.* And it was just the clue I needed.

I looked at Woofer's feet. They were dirty. I thought about what Dad had said. He'd called Woofer a thief. A thief stole things, and Greenie had been stolen!

Woofer looked at me and scratched. The scratching made his collar jingle. Tiana had said she'd heard jingle bells at nap time. She hadn't been dreaming after all. She'd heard Woofer's collar.

"Woofer!" I shouted. "Woofer stole Greenie!"

Tiana's eyes got big. "Woofer?"

I nodded. "Look at his dirty feet! And did you hear how his collar jingled when he scratched?" I was finally about to solve the mystery! "And Auntie Sam just said he buries stuff in the garden. That's where we need to be searching. Greenie is out there somewhere!"

Tiana got up and clapped. "Yay! Find Greenie! Find Greenie!"

Everybody ran outside. Woofer came with us too. He wagged his tail and almost looked like he was smiling. Woofer thought this whole thing was funny.

I knew we needed a strategy. We couldn't just dig holes all over the garden. That would take too long. It would also make Mum and Dad cross.

"Let's spread out," I said. "Look for places where the ground doesn't look normal. Like piles of soil or little holes."

I went to the far side of the garden and started searching. I found a spot that didn't look right. I brushed the soil to the side and found Woofer's ball. Woofer barked at me and wagged his tail.

"Azaleah!" shouted Tiana. "Come and see!"

I hurried over to where Tiana stood next to a loose pile of soil. I poked a finger into the ground to see if I could feel anything and touched something soft. I pulled it out.

"Woofer *stealed* Mum's sock?" said Tiana.

"Looks like Woofer's been busy," Dad said.

Before long, everybody was running around pulling things out of the ground. Woofer had stolen a spoon, a paintbrush and Nia's wig from her last musical.

Finally, I found a big pile of soil under one

of the bushes. I had to put my whole head under the bush to dig. There was definitely something under there, but I couldn't reach it.

"Tiana, come and help me!" I yelled.

Tiana came running. "Did you find Greenie?" she asked.

"I don't know," I said. "You're smaller than me. You have to go under there and dig."

Tiana got on her stomach and crawled under the bush. I watched her legs wiggle while she dug.

"Greenie!" she yelled. She scooted back out of the bush, clutching Greenie in one hand.

Leaves were stuck in Tiana's hair. Both she and her toy were filthy, but Tiana didn't seem to care. She and Greenie gave me a big hug.

They got me dirty, but I laughed and hugged them back. Everybody cheered.

"Me and Greenie are going to have a bath," said Tiana. She ran inside.

Woofer licked my hand and barked.

"I think Woofer needs a time-out," Auntie Sam said. "Sorry about the garden."

Dad shook his head and smiled at me. "Good job, Detective Azaleah." He kissed me. "You'd better go and finish that model."

"I was just thinking the same thing," I said.

CHAPTER 10

MISSION COMPLETE

I got to work on my model. I collected plants from our garden. I decided to use little branches from the bush Greenie had been hiding under. They would be the bushes and trees in the tiger habitat. Once I had enough, I ran upstairs to finish my project.

I crossed step four off my list, since I had already collected plants. Next, I painted my tiger. It had to dry before I could stick everything onto the box. But now that the mystery was solved, I had the rest of the day to let it sit on my desk.

While I was cutting out some paper grass, there was a knock on my door. I hoped it wasn't Tiana. This time I was going to make her keep her promise to leave me alone.

"Who is it?" I asked.

"Mum."

I was relieved. "Come in," I said.

Mum was holding a white plate with a gigantic white mug sitting on it. It was

her famous gourmet hot chocolate. Everyone loved Mum's hot chocolate. It had secret ingredients. They were so secret she wouldn't even tell us what they were.

"I made this especially for you," Mum said, putting it on my desk. She had even put a big swirl of whipped cream on top.

I gave Mum a hug, took a sip and said, "Ahhhh."

Mum sat on my bed and watched me work. I sipped hot chocolate and cut the paper grass. After a while, Mum tiptoed back to the door.

"I love you, Azaleah Lane. You're amazing," she said.

I smiled at Mum. "I love you too."

I stayed in my room and worked on my model for the rest of the day. By the time I had cut the grass and stuck all of the plants on the model, my tiger was dry.

I added some extra touches too. I crumpled up a strip of dark-green tissue paper to make a swampy river, since tigers were really good swimmers. Then I got a piece of lined paper and cut out a little rectangle. I wrote some important tiger facts on it:

- Tigers are critically endangered.
- They only live on seven per cent of what used to be their native habitat.
- They can be found in Russia, Sumatra, China and other parts of Asia.
- They can live in forests, near swamps and on grasslands.
- The zoo is trying to help save the tigers.

I glued the paper on top of my model. Then I stuck Nikita in the middle of her habitat. My extra touches were really good. The model looked just like I wanted it to.

It was impressive. At least, I thought so. Hopefully, Mrs Li would think so too.

* * *

On Monday morning, I walked very carefully up the steps to my school. I walked so slowly that I barely made it to my classroom before the bell rang.

"Good morning, boys and girls," said Miss Johnson. "If you have a model, put it on the shelf and sit down."

I walked over and put my model down on the bookshelf. Six others were already there – I counted five pandas and one naked mole rat. Everyone had done a nice job, but I was the only one with a tiger *and* the only one with a list of facts.

Rose came over and put her model down on the shelf too. She had made a very

impressive panda habitat. It was the best panda of all.

"Wow," Rose whispered, looking at my model. "That's really good. I bet you're going to get *congratulations* and *recognitions*."

"Thank you," I whispered.

I walked to my seat, grinning all the way. I hoped Rose was right, but either way I was proud of my model *and* my amazing mystery-solving skills. Now I could finally relax . . . until there was another mystery to solve, of course!

About the author

Nikki Shannon Smith is from Oakland, California USA. She lives with her husband and two children. She is a primary school teacher and she writes everything from picture books to young adult novels. Her books include *The Little Christmas Elf*, *Treasure Hunt*, *Ann Fights for Freedom: An Underground Railroad Survival Story* and *Noelle at Sea: A Titanic Survival Story*. When she's not busy with family, work or writing, Nikki loves to go to the sea. The first thing she packs in her suitcase is always a book.

About the illustrator

Mari Lobo was born and raised in Sao Paulo, Brazil, where she spent her childhood playing on the streets and climbing trees. She was always fond of drawing and painting, and by the age of fifteen she decided to be an artist. After completing a degree in industrial design she worked in the fashion industry for a few years. Mari then moved to California, USA, where she gained a master's degree in visual development for animation. She lives with her classical musician husband. They like to go to concerts, on hikes and to dinner with friends. But mostly she sits in front of her computer and draws for children all day, every day because she loved being a child herself.

Glossary

audition an interview for a role or job as a singer, actor, musician or dancer

conservation the protection of animals and plants

elimination the act or process of getting rid of something

endangered in danger of dying out

habitat the natural place and conditions in which a plant or animal lives

hypothesis a prediction that can be tested about how a scientific investigation or experiment will turn out

nocturnal active at night and resting during the day

recognition special attention or notice

sachet a small bag that has a powder or mixture of dried flowers and spices inside it. It is used to give a pleasant smell to clothes, sheets, etc.

species a group of plants or animals that share common characteristics

strategy a careful plan or method

suspect someone who may be responsible for a crime

vulnerable in a weak position and likely to be hurt or damaged in some way

Let's talk!

1. Azaleah and her sisters, Nia and Tiana, are all very different. If you could choose one of the Lane girls to be your sister, which would you choose? Why? Talk about the qualities that made you choose that person.

2. Tiana completely ruined Lazy Saturday with the hunt for Greenie. Do you think she should have been allowed to have a sleepover with Azaleah? Talk about why or why not.

3. This story ends before we find out if Azaleah gets congratulations and recognitions from her headteacher, Mrs Li, for her model. What do you think happens after the last chapter? Talk about what you think might happen when Mrs Li sees Azaleah's work.

4. Azaleah searched for Greenie in many places both inside and outside their house. Talk about all the places she searched. Can you get them in the right order? Feel free to look back through the story for help.

Let's write!

1. Azaleah is torn between a tiger and a panda for her model, but Woofer might be the most important animal in this book. If he could talk, what do you think he'd say? Use your imagination to pretend you are Woofer. Write a letter to either Tiana or Azaleah about what happened.

2. At the end of the book, Azaleah says she has amazing mystery-solving skills. Do you agree or disagree? Write a paragraph explaining your answer. Use at least three details from the book for support.

3. Pick an animal that you might find at a zoo, and write a paragraph teaching others about it. Include three to five details about your animal, such as its natural habitat, what it eats and other interesting facts. Try to find out if your animal is vulnerable, endangered or critically endangered.

4. Azaleah makes lists to help her get her work done. Think of a big job you need to finish. It can be homework, a project or a chore at home, like cleaning your room. Make a list of all of the steps you will take to finish the job.

Make your own model scene

You can make a model just like Azaleah's! To get started, choose and research an animal. There are lots of resources you can use. You can visit a zoo in person, look at library books about your animal or you can visit some zoo's websites.

Pay attention to your animal's habitat. What kinds of plants grow there? Is it a wet habitat, a dry habitat or somewhere in between? Are there mountains, rivers or lakes? Does your animal like to live alone or with a group? What is its source of food? Next, think about what your animal looks like. Is it big or small? Is it furry or scaly?

Once you know all about your animal and its habitat, you're ready to create a model habitat. Be creative. You might have lots of things already at home to use for this project!

What you need:

- medium-sized box (shoeboxes work well)
- paint
- plants (real ones from outside or fake ones from an art shop or garden centre) for your habitat
- paper, cardboard or modelling clay to make your animal
- liquid glue or a glue stick
- crayons, marker pens or coloured pencils

- any extra supplies (like string, tissue paper, rocks or soil) you have to make your model amazing
- lined paper

What to do:

1. Paint the outside of your box or cover it with paper.
2. Begin making the inside of your box look like your animal's habitat. You can start by painting the sky blue or the grass green.
3. Create or collect plants and other natural features for your habitat. Glue them into your box. Make sure all the things your animal needs to hide, eat and survive are in the scene.
4. Next, make your animal. You can draw and colour it on paper or cardboard. Then, cut it out. You could also shape it out of modelling clay. Paint it if needed.
5. Glue your animal into its habitat.
6. When you're finished, write a list of facts about your animal on lined paper. Attach it to the outside of your model, just like Azaleah.

Oh, and if you have a younger sibling, like Tiana, keep her or him away from your finished project!

THE FUN DOESN'T STOP HERE!

DISCOVER MORE AUTHORS, ILLUSTRATORS AND BOOKS AT

WWW.RAINTREE.CO.UK